The WRONG-WAY RABBIT

by Teddy Slater
Illustrated by Diane de Groat

Hello Reader!—Level 2

SCHOLASTIC INC.

Cartwheel B·O·O·K·S·®

New York   London   Toronto   Auckland   Sydney

A NOTE TO PARENTS

Reading Aloud with Your Child
Research shows that reading books aloud is the single most valuable support parents can provide in helping children learn to read.
- Be a ham! The more enthusiasm you display, the more your child will enjoy the book.
- Run your finger underneath the words as you read to signal that the print carries the story.
- Leave time for examining the illustrations more closely; encourage your child to find things in the pictures.
- Invite your youngster to join in whenever there's a repeated phrase in the text.
- Link up events in the book with similar events in your child's life.
- If your child asks a question, stop and answer it. The book can be a means to learning more about your child's thoughts.

Listening to Your Child Read Aloud
The support of your attention and praise is absolutely crucial to your child's continuing efforts to learn to read.
- If your child is learning to read and asks for a word, give it immediately so that the meaning of the story is not interrupted. DO NOT ask your child to sound out the word.
- On the other hand, if your child initiates the act of sounding out, don't intervene.
- If your child is reading along and makes what is called a miscue, listen for the sense of the miscue. If the word "road" is substituted for the word "street," for instance, no meaning is lost. Don't stop the reading for a correction.
- If the miscue makes no sense (for example, "horse" for "house"), ask your child to reread the sentence because you're not sure you understand what's just been read.
- Above all else, enjoy your child's growing command of print and make sure you give lots of praise. *You are your child's first teacher—and the most important one. Praise from you is critical for further risk-taking and learning.*

—Priscilla Lynch
Ph.D., New York University
Educational Consultant

For Ykceb and Alil Seilugram — T.S.

Text Copyright © 1993 by Teddy Slater.
Illustrations copyright © 1993 by Diane de Groat.
All rights reserved. Published by Scholastic Inc.
HELLO READER!, CARTWHEEL BOOKS, and the CARTWHEEL BOOKS
logo are registered trademarks of Scholastic Inc.

Library of Congress Cataloging-in-Publication Data

Slater, Teddy.
    The Wrong-Way Rabbit / by Teddy Slater: illustrated by Diane de Groat.
       p.   cm. — (Hello reader)
    Summary: Tibbar the backward bunny does everything the opposite
from what's expected, walking backwards and going up the down stairs.
    ISBN 0-590-45359-9
    [1. Rabbits — Fiction. 2. Individuality — Fiction. 3. Stories in rhyme.]
I. de Groat, Diane, ill. II. Title. III. Series.
PZ8.3.S6318Bac   1993
[E] — dc20   92-14334
                                                       CIP
                                                       AC

ISBN 0-590-45359-9

19 18 17 16 15 14 13   6 7 8/9

Printed in the U.S.A.   **24**

First Scholastic printing, February 1993

Chapter 1
HERE COMES TIBBAR JACK

Hippity-hop,
it's Tibbar Jack,
a very mixed-up bunny.

The way he walks
is sort of strange.

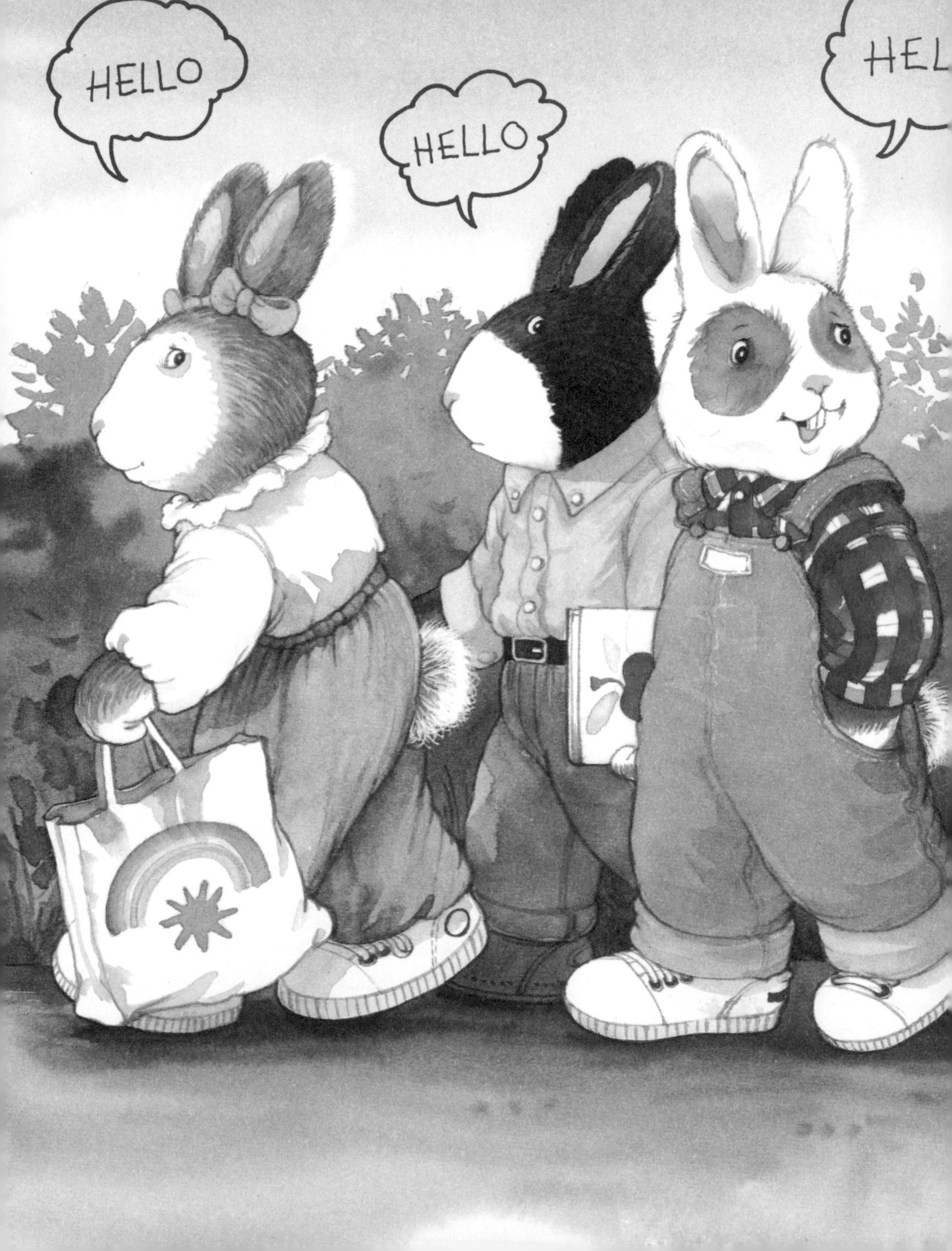

The way he talks is funny.

"Good night!" he sings out every day,
just as the sun comes up.

He pours his juice into his bowl,
his cornflakes in his cup.

Jack wears his sweater inside out.

His socks go on his ears.
Of course, he can't
hear much that way. . . .

It drives his mom to tears.

"Go to town and buy some oats,"
his mother said one day.

But Tibbar did not hear her right. . . .

What else is there to say?

Chapter 2
T. J. GOES TO SCHOOL

Tickity-tock!
It's eight o'clock —
time to go to school.

Sometimes Jack acts silly,
but this bunny is no fool.

ZYXW

T.J. knows his CBA's.

V U T S R Q P O N

Hear him count to ten:
"Thirteen, twelve, eleven, ten . . ."

20 19 18 17 16

20 19 18 17 16

and then he starts again.

15 14 13 12 11 10

15 14

In the **OUT** door Tibbar goes . . .

up the stairs marked **DOWN**.

He always paints his cows bright blue.
He makes his skies light brown.

When everybody cuts and pastes,
Tibbar pastes and cuts.

He likes to do things his own way.
It drives his teacher nuts.

Chapter 3
GOOD NIGHT, TIBBAR JACK

Rub-a-dub-dub
and into the tub,
Jack steps with all his clothes.

When he is wet,
he gets undressed.
That's how his bath time goes.

At seven-thirty on the dot,
Mom tucks her son in bed.

But Tibbar never sleeps at night.
He'd rather play instead.

Jack likes his story back to front,
the end before the start.
That way he knows how things turn out.
It makes him feel quite smart.

Inside out and upside down,
Jack's always looking back.
Things sure can get confusing
when your name is Tibbar Jack.

Yes, living life the way Jack does
is more than just a habit.
And if you haven't guessed it yet . . .

spelled backwards
he's Jack Rabbit!